THE LEGEND OF ROCK PAPER SCISSORS

DREW DAYWALT ADAM REX

HarperCollins *Children's Books*

To my champions,
Roger Di Paolo
Tom Stephan
Rose Mary Piazza Stehman-Humble

— D.D.

For Henry

— A.R.

GO!

First published in hardback in the USA by Balzer and Bray,
an imprint of HarperCollins *Publishers*, in 2017
First published in hardback in Great Britain by HarperCollins *Children's Books* in 2017
First published in paperback by HarperCollins *Children's Books* in 2018

5 7 9 10 8 6

ISBN: 978-0-00-825263-2

HarperCollins *Children's Books* is a division of HarperCollins *Publishers* Ltd.

Text copyright © Drew Daywalt 2017
Illustrations copyright © Adam Rex 2017
Typography by Adam Rex and Dana Fritts

Visit our website at: www.harpercollins.co.uk

Printed and bound in China

Long ago,

in an ancient and distant realm called
the Kingdom of Backgarden,

there lived a warrior named
ROCK.

Rock was the strongest in
all the land, but he was
sad because no one could
give him a worthy challenge.

Rock travelled to
the mysterious Forest
of Over by the Tyre Swing,
where he met a warrior
who hung on a rope,
holding a giant's underwear.

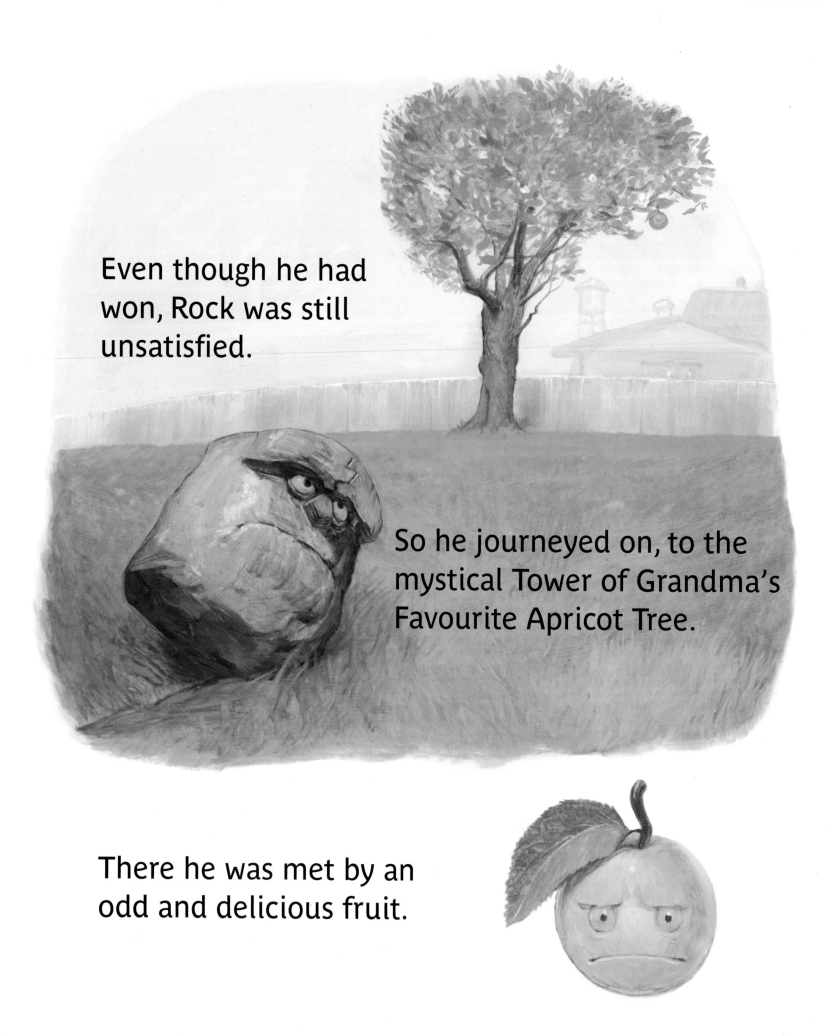

Even though he had won, Rock was still unsatisfied.

So he journeyed on, to the mystical Tower of Grandma's Favourite Apricot Tree.

There he was met by an odd and delicious fruit.

ROCK IS VICTORIOUS!

Ugh, I am smooshed!

AND YET, SMOOSHING YOU HAS BROUGHT ME NO JOY.

They *were* entertained.

But the battle had been too easy. So Rock left the Kingdom of Backgarden, still in search of a worthy foe.

Meanwhile,
in the Empire of Mum's Study, on lonely and windswept Desk Mountain, a second great warrior sought the glory of battle.

And his name was Paper.

Even though he was the cleverest warrior in all the land, he was also sad, because no one could outwit him.

He set out across Desk Mountain to find his match. There he met a large and square monster.

Paper versus Computer Printer!

Having beaten the fiercest fighter
of Desk Mountain, Paper climbed
down to the Pit of Office Rubbish Bin,
where he battled the most terrifying
horde of creatures in all the land . . .

the HALF-EATEN BAG OF TRAIL MIX!

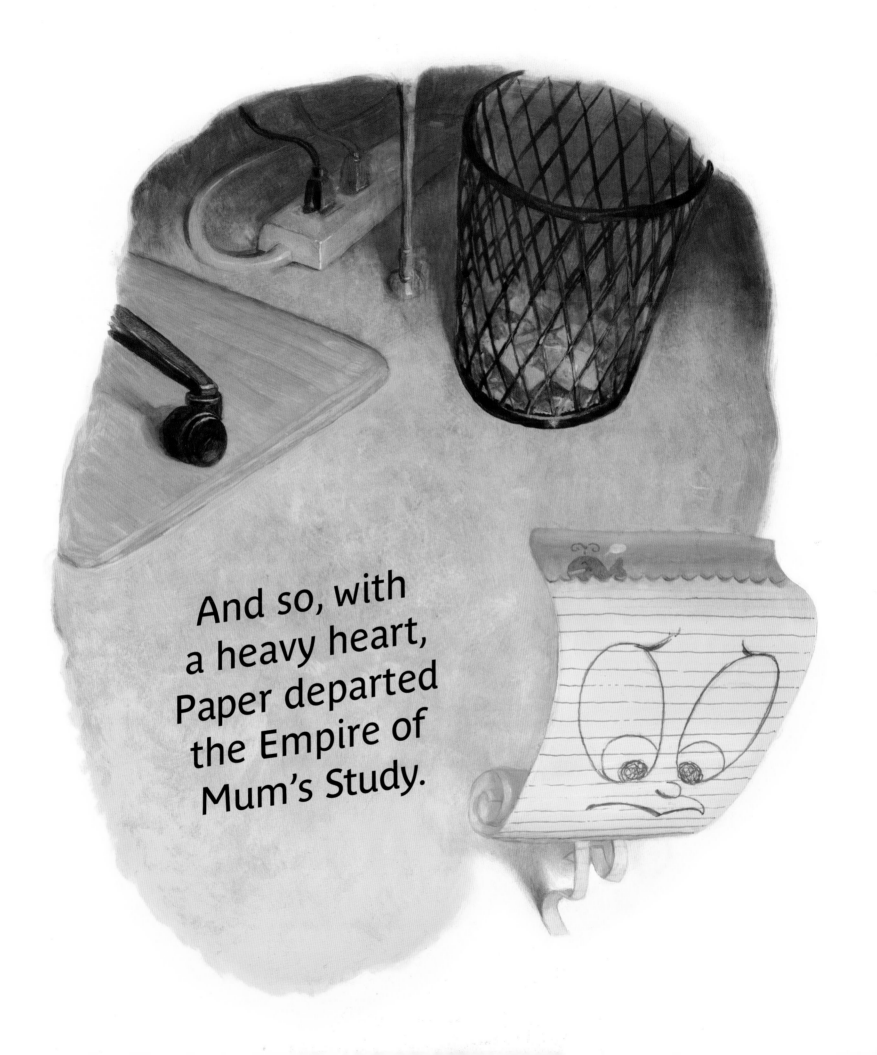

And so, with
a heavy heart,
Paper departed
the Empire of
Mum's Study.

At the same time,

in the Kitchen Realm,

in the tiny village of Junk Drawer,
there lived a third great warrior.

They called her Scissors,

and she was the fastest blade in
all the land. She, too, was unchallenged.
On this day, her first opponent was a
strange and sticky circle-man.

Scissors forged on across the Kitchen Realm
to the frigid wastes of Refrigerator/Freezer.
There she met her most fearsome adversaries yet . . .
dinosaurs made of frozen breaded chicken.

AM I SO GOOD THAT NOT EVEN DINOSAUR-SHAPED CHICKEN NUGGETS CAN BEAT ME?

And so Scissors, like Rock and Paper before her, travelled beyond her own kingdom, seeking out a challenger who was her equal.

Then one day,
in the great cavern
of Two-Car Garage,

Rock and Scissors
came face-to-face.

I hope you're wearing your battle pants, rock warrior.

IF BY "BATTLE PANTS" YOU MEAN "NO PANTS, BUT I'M WILLING TO FIGHT YOU," THEN YES . . . YES, I AM WEARING MY BATTLE PANTS, WEIRD SCISSORY ONE!

An epic
and legendary battle
ensued, but ultimately . . .

ROCK
IS VICTORIOUS!

And the three great warriors hugged each other and danced for joy, and they became best friends.

Finally, they had each met their matches. They were so happy, in fact, that they began to battle again.

Round and round they went, in the most massive and epic three-way battle of all time! And it is said that this joyous struggle still rages on to this very day.

That is why children around the world – in back gardens, on playgrounds, and yes, even in classrooms – still honour the three great warriors by playing . . .